CH00055379

Before reading

Look at the book cov...
Ask, "What do you thi...

Turn to the **Key Word** ...
the child. Draw their ...ng
the tall letters and tho...

During reading

Offer plenty of support and praise as the child reads the story.
Listen carefully and respond to events in the text.

When a **Key Word** is used for the first time, it is also shown at
the bottom of the page. If the child hesitates over a word, point
to the **New Key Words** box and practise reading it together.
If the word is phonically decodable, you can sound out the
letters and blend the sounds to read the word ("d-o-g, dog").
Praise the child for their effort, then return to the story.

Pause every few pages and ask questions to check the child's
understanding of what they have read. If they begin to lose
concentration, stop reading and save the page for later.

Celebrate the child's achievement and come back to the
story the next day.

After reading

After reading this book, ask, "Did you enjoy the story? What did
you like about it?" Encourage the child to share their opinions.

Use the comprehension questions on page 54 to check the
child's understanding and recall of the text.

Ladybird

Series Consultant: Professor David Waugh
With thanks to Kulwinder Maude

LADYBIRD BOOKS

UK | USA | Canada | Ireland | Australia
India | New Zealand | South Africa

Ladybird Books is part of the Penguin Random House group of companies
whose addresses can be found at global.penguinrandomhouse.com.
www.penguin.co.uk   www.puffin.co.uk   www.ladybird.co.uk

Penguin
Random House
UK

Original edition of Key Words with Peter and Jane first published by Ladybird Books Ltd 1964
Series updated 2023
This book first published 2023
001

With thanks to Liz Pemberton for her contributions in advising on the illustrations
With thanks to Inclusive Minds for connecting us with their Inclusion Ambassador network,
and in particular thanks to Guntaas Kaur Chugh for her input on the illustrations

Printed in China

The authorized representative in the EEA is Penguin Random House Ireland,
Morrison Chambers, 32 Nassau Street, Dublin D02 YH68

A CIP catalogue record for this book is available from the British Library

ISBN: 978-0-241-51082-7

All correspondence to:
Ladybird Books
Penguin Random House Children's
One Embassy Gardens, 8 Viaduct Gardens, London SW11 7BW

MIX
Paper from
responsible sources
FSC® C018179

Key Words

with Peter and Jane

4a

We have fun

Based on the original
Key Words with Peter and Jane
reading scheme and research by William Murray

Original edition written by William Murray
This edition written by Shari Last
Illustrated by Gustavo Mazali

bear bed boat

boy children down

friend fruit girl

give good help

me one red

school see some

station tea train

up was

bear

bed

boat

boy

children

down

fruit

girl

school

station

tea

train

up

7

Peter and Jane go up and down.

"Up, up, up," says Peter.

"Down, down, down," says Jane.

Up and down.

"A boat! Come on the boat," says Jane.

Peter likes boats.

"This is a good boat," he says.

Jane sees some
red boats.

"Look at the red boats,
Peter!" says Jane.

"I can see some. They
are on the water,"
says Peter.

New Key Words

    see   some   red

Here is the dog. Tess sees the children in the boat.

"Can we have some fruit?" says Jane.

"Yes," says Peter.

Peter has some rock buns. He gives Jane one. He gives some to Mum and Dad.

Jane gives Peter some fruit.

"The fruit is good," says Peter.

"We can get the train home," says Mum.

"I see the train!" says Jane.

The children go up to the train station.

The train at the station is red.

"I like red trains," says Peter.

"And me!" says Jane.

Jane is on the bed.

The bed is red.

She jumps up and
down on the red bed.

New Key Words

bed

23

The children go to bed.

Peter is in bed
with Bear.

"Me and Bear. Bear
and me," says Peter.

The children see Mum
with some tools.

"Can we help, Mum?"
says Jane.

"I like helping,"
says Peter.

"You are good at
helping," says Mum.

New Key Words

help

"That one goes up
here" says Mum.

"This one?" says Peter.

"Yes. Good boy,"
says Mum.

The children help
Dad to cook.

"Look at me, Dad!"
says Jane.

"Look at me! Me, me,
me!" says Peter.

The children are good helpers. They like helping Dad with tea.

"Can you give me some fruit, Jane?" says Peter.

"This tea looks good, Dad," says Jane.

33

Dad gives the children some fruit.

"I like the red fruits," says Jane.

"And me!" says Peter.

Jane is in the red bed.
She was a good girl.

She helped Mum.

She helped Dad.

"Helping was fun,"
says Peter.

Peter hugs Bear in bed.

"Bear and I are good
friends," he says.

New Key Words

friend

39

The children go to
Red Tree School.

"I like school,"
says Peter.

"And me! We see
friends at school,"
says Jane.

New Key Words

school

The children see some friends at Red Tree School.

Amber is Peter's good friend.

Pippa and Will are Jane's good friends.

The boys and girls play at school.

Amber gives the red ball to Peter.

"Give me the red ball," says Jane.

Some boys and girls
from school come
for tea.

Mum gives the children
some fruit.

"I like tea with friends,"
says Jane.

The boys and girls help Dad.

"Just one cup to go," says Dad.

"This one?" says Peter.

49

"See you," says Jane.

"That was good,"
says Peter.

The boys and girls
go home.

"School was good,"
says Jane.

"Tea was good,"
says Peter.

"And bed is good!
Up you go," says Mum.

53

Questions

**Answer these questions about
the story.**

1 What do Peter and Jane see
on the water?

2 How do Peter and Jane get home
from the beach?

3 How do Peter and Jane help Mum
and Dad at home?

4 What do the children do
after school?